709

Artists' Workshop

Stories

Penny King & Clare Roundhill

A & C Black · London

Designed by **Jane Warring**

Illustrations by **Lindy Norton**

Children's pictures by
**Amber Civardi, Charlotte Downham, Lara Haworth,
Lucinda Howell, Sophie Johns, Julia Luther,
Lucy MacDonald Watson, India Masson-Taylor,
Zoë More O'Ferrall, Gussie Pownall, Thomas Stofer,
Alice Williams, Jessica Williams**

Photographs by **Peter Millard**

Picture Research **by Sara Elliott**

First published in 1996 by
A & C Black (Publishers) Limited
35 Bedford Row, London WC1R 4JH

Created by
Thumbprint Books

Copyright © 1996 Thumbprint Books

A CIP catalogue record for this book is available from the British Library

ISBN 0-7136-4184-3

Printed and bound in Singapore

Cover Photograph: The Harvest, 1989, is a Peruvian *Arpillera* (appliqué).
Women throughout Latin America make embroidery
pictures, like this, to tell stories about their life
in villages and on farms. Women's organisations sell them
to help raise money for their communities.

Contents

Story pictures

Long ago, most people did not learn to read and write. Instead, they listened to stories and learned about ideas and events from what other people told them, or through pictures.

The Ancient Greeks illustrated scenes from myths on vases and plates, and carved the heroes in marble and wood.

In the Middle Ages, people in Europe were taught about the Bible through the stories carved in stone around the entrance to churches, or on the stained-glass windows inside.

In India, several hundred years ago, storytellers travelled from village to village with an illustrated scroll that unfolded to show scenes from great epics. In the East, epic stories were often performed as puppet plays.

In many cases, stories were illustrated on walls, rugs, tapestries, cups and plates and even on clothes. Today, you can read stories in books or watch them on television or at the cinema. All kinds of stories are also told in cartoons.

Ballets and operas also tell exciting stories. Music and mime help to explain the plots which are sometimes quite long and complicated.

Pictures can say as much, if not more, than words. The six main pictures in this book each tell a wonderful story. There is the embroidered story of a real battle that took place almost a thousand years ago; a Russian fairy tale about a frog princess and the brave prince who rescued her; a magical tale of love and confusion by Shakespeare; an ancient Indian saga about a royal prince and a wicked demon.

There is also a fable painted on a plate and the enchanting story of Cinderella.

You may find that the pictures which illustrate these stories don't match up with the ones you have in your head.

Use all the techniques shown in the book to illustrate your versions of these stories and then try creating pictures of your own favourite stories.

Battleground bravery

The Bayeux Tapestry was sewn by skilled needlewomen, using many different stitches, but only eight colours. It would probably take days, or even weeks, to draw all the people, animals and events it shows. Here are several different ways of making your own Bayeux-style pictures.

Stitched shield

Make a coloured sketch of a shield like one of those used by the soldiers in the tapestry. Design a bold pattern or fancy initials for it, or draw a picture of a fierce animal to frighten away enemies. Stitch the outline of your shield on a square of felt. Sew the details in different coloured threads and stitches.

Colossal collage

Make a collage of a fierce battle scene. Use a large piece of pale felt for the background. Cut out soldiers with felt faces and shiny fabric armour. Stick on felt eyes and mouths and any other details. Use fleecy or furry material for horses and stick on woolly manes and tails.

Glue everything on to the background and then add cocktail stick spears and flagpoles.

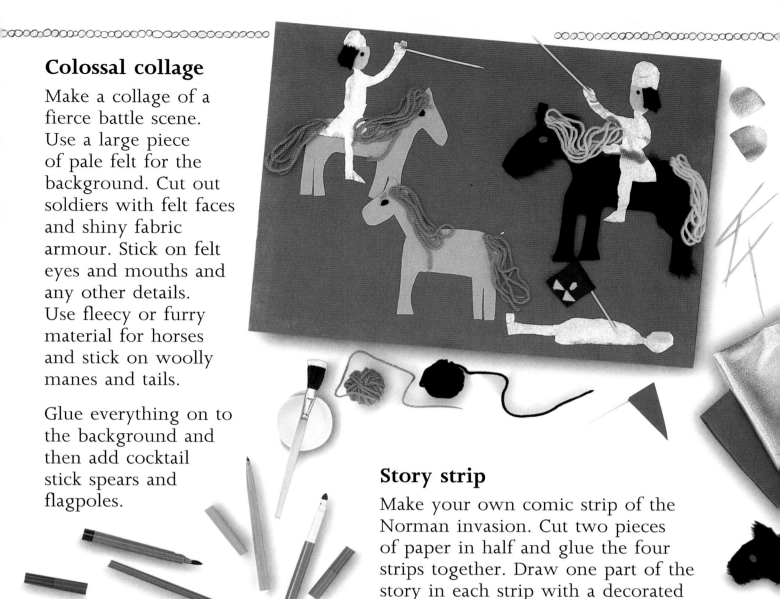

Story strip

Make your own comic strip of the Norman invasion. Cut two pieces of paper in half and glue the four strips together. Draw one part of the story in each strip with a decorated border along the top and bottom.

An Indian epic

The Ramayana is an ancient and famous
Indian saga. Centuries ago, this long
and exciting tale about Rama,
a blue-skinned prince, was told by
storytellers. In the 3rd century BC,
a poet called Valmiki wrote it down.
Later, the story was shown in exquisitely
detailed pictures so that people who
could not read could follow the tale.

Sanskrit illumination for the Ramayana, The British Library, London

There are over 400 pictures in the
series that this painting comes from.
Often a team of artists worked for
years on the illustrations for rich
kings. The master artist sketched
each drawing and lesser artists
filled in the colours.

This picture shows the part of the
story when Rama was living in the
forest. He is having a meal with his
wife, Princess Sita, and his brother,
Lakshmana. Bows and arrows hang
on the hut ready for the two princes
to go out hunting for deer.

Rama's story

A long time ago, in India, there lived a prince, called Rama. His jealous stepmother had him banished because she wanted her own son to be the next king. For 14 years, Rama lived deep in the forest with his wife, Princess Sita, and his brother, Lakshmana.

One day an evil ten-headed demon, called Ravana, sent a golden deer to lure Prince Rama away from Sita.

Ravana kidnapped the princess and flew off with her in his chariot. On the way to the demon's palace on the island of Lanka, Sita threw out her jewels hoping that Rama would find them and come to rescue her.

Rama and Lakshmana searched all over India until they came to the land of the monkeys. They made friends with Hanuman, the monkey leader, who found Sita's jewels and told Rama where she was being held captive.

With the help of the monkeys, Rama and Lakshmana built a bridge across the dangerous sea and marched to Lanka. After days and nights of fierce battle, Rama killed Ravana and rescued his faithful Princess Sita.

At last it was time for Rama to return home and take his place as king. His loyal subjects lit hundreds of oil lamps to guide their hero back to his kingdom.

Devilish tricks

Imagine what Ravana, the evil demon, looked like and then create one or all of his ten ugly heads. Or you might like to paint or print a delicately patterned picture of the part of Prince Rama's story that you enjoyed the most.

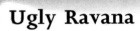

Ugly Ravana

Draw the outline of one of Ravana's ugly heads on a piece of stiff card. Mix a sickly shade of green poster paint and add some flour to make it really thick. Paint the head with the mixture and let it dry.

Paint or glue hideous features on to the face. You could use scrunched-up tissue paper for eyes, a lavatory roll for the nose, a sponge for a lolling tongue, silver foil for horns and black wool for hair.

Indian images

Use felt-tip pens, paints or crayons, to illustrate any part of Prince Rama's story. Fill the paper with bright colours, busy figures and animals. Use lots of delicate patterns for the leaves, clothes and flowers.

Printed princess

Collect several different things for making prints, such as a cork, sponge, kitchen cloth, potato cuts or cauliflower florets cut in half. Using poster paints, practise printing with each one to see what different shapes and textures they make.

Now create a printed picture — maybe of Princess Sita in a beautiful dress wearing her jewels, or the furry monkeys helping Rama to build the bridge. When the paint is dry, outline the figures in black.

13

Blue and white pictures

Imagine, like Koong Shee, that you have entered the blue and white world of the willow pattern. Use the ideas of the original story or make up your own, to create a plate painted with pictures and patterns.

Painted plates

Decide which parts of the willow pattern story you want to show and then draw them in pencil on a white card circle. Draw a patterned border around the edge.

Put blue and white paint on to a palette, or into two separate pots. Mix a little of each in different amounts to make all sorts of shades of blue. The more white you add, the paler the blue will become. Paint your story, using a fine-tipped paintbrush so you can put in lots of details and patterns.

Other things to do

1 Cut a card circle and decorate it with stickers. Cut some big white card petals. On each one, paint an exciting or important thing that has happened to you. Start with the day you were born. Stick the petals, in order, clockwise around the centre of the flower, so that they tell the story of your life.

3 Choose one of your favourite stories or make up a story of your own. Try to tell the story in one picture, rather like the willow pattern story. Include pictures of each of the places and people in the story. You might like to draw your story on a paper plate and decorate the edge with a patterned border.

2 Design an information poster without any words, so that it could be understood by people all over the world. You could explain the safe way to cross a road, how to look after pets, or why it is important to brush your teeth every day. Draw several pictures to get your message across clearly.

4 Create your own storybook, by putting eight strips of paper one on top of the other. Fold them in half and sew them together along the fold. Write part of a story on each page. Illustrate them, using a different technique for each one, such as paint, wax resist, silhouette and collage. Design an eye-catching cover.

Index

Acknowledgements

The publishers are grateful to the following institutes and individuals for permission to reproduce the illustrations on the pages mentioned.
The Harvest, 1989, Peruvian Arpillera, kindly lent by Sandy Adirondack: cover; The Bayeux Tapestry - 11th Century. By special permission of the City of Bayeux: 6; Sanskrit illumination for the Ramayana, The British Library, London (15296F.71r): 10; Spode willow pattern plate, by courtesy of Spode, Stoke-on-Trent: 14; Marc Chagall, Midsummer Night's Dream, 1939, Musée de Grenoble / © ADAGP, Paris and DACS, London, 1996: 22; Yagodkina, Russian Miniature Box, 1992, Iconastas, London: 26.